Bog Dog's Beach Adventure

Written and Illustrated by

Kate Walls

Printed in the USA by Sir Speedy
180 Rte. 6A #2, Orleans, MA 02653
ISBN: 978-0-615-61431-1

Library of Congress Control Number: 2012904622

There is nothing better than stretching in the morning sun. It is going to be a beautiful summer day.

As Skipper was sitting by the edge of the bog, he noticed the osprey fly off to catch fish for his family's breakfast. Skipper had always wondered where the osprey went fishing.

Skipper thought, "Today is the perfect day for an adventure." He jumped up and ran to the edge of the bog where he could still see the osprey flying away. Skipper ran past the bog and through the woods.

He was so busy following the osprey, he didn't notice he was standing on the edge of the marsh. His paws started to sink into the mud. It was really smelly and he... loved it. He jumped around pouncing deeper into the mud.

Off to the side of the marsh he noticed small things running around. He ran over to see what they were and they all scurried into holes. Skipper kept sniffing trying to figure out what they were.

Finally one of the fiddler crabs climbed out of his hole and said "Go away little doggie!" Skipper noticed other crabs starting to climb out of their holes. He thought maybe he would listen to the crabby crab and went on his way.

Skipper ran along the edge of the marsh where he saw a great blue heron. It was so still, it looked like a statue. In a flash the heron plunged his head into the water.

He came up with a fish in his bill. He threw back his head and quickly gulped down the fish. As the heron went back to fishing, Skipper ran until he came to a sandy beach.

Skipper looked down and noticed little periwinkles. With his paw he rolled over one of the snails. The periwinkle closed up tightly, safe into it's shell.

Just then the tide washed a big old horseshoe crab closer to shore. She said "Pardon me, but I need to get back in the water before the tide goes out. I don't want to be out on the sand". Within seconds, she was gone.

CRUNCH!! SMASH!! "What was that?" Skipper looked behind him. He noticed smashed shells. He looked up and saw a seagull dropping a spider crab from the sky. "What are you doing Mr. Gull?"

The seagulls started to eat out of the broken shells. One of the seagulls said, "This is how we open our lunch. We drop it onto something hard and it breaks open. Yum - want some?" Skipper said "No thank you." He didn't think it looked yummy at all.

The tide was going out quickly and sandbars were popping up. Skipper noticed squirts of water coming up from the sand. "What is that?" He ran over to the little hole and got squirted in the face. He dug into the hole until he pulled out a clam.

The clam said, "Hey dude! Put me back and cover me up! My home is deep in the sand." Skipper apologized and happily covered up the clam.

Skipper looked down the beach. He saw little plovers zig zagging along the shore line. He wondered if they were afraid of the water. "Why do you run from the waves?" Skipper asked.

The plover said, "My legs are a lot shorter than yours. The waves can knock us over. We like to run close to them because we find delicious snacks to eat." With the next wave they were off and running down the beach.

As the plovers ran off, Skipper looked along the wrack line to see if there was anything good for him to eat. He found many beautiful shells and lots of sticky seaweed.

Skipper then went into the shallow water. He noticed something was moving very slowly. It was a moon snail. He also spotted minnows swimming quickly to avoid getting caught in the waves and pushed onto the shore.

Skipper looked up and noticed the osprey flying back and forth. Suddenly the osprey dove into the water.

Just as quickly, he burst out of the water. He had a big fish in his claws. Skipper thought, "That will make a nice meal for the osprey's family."

While watching the osprey fly away, Skipper realized the osprey was heading home. "Oh no! I have to get back to the bog!" Skipper jumped up and ran down the beach.

He ran into the marsh, through the woods and over to the bog. By the time Skipper got home, the osprey and his family had already eaten their fish and he was flying off to catch another.

Skipper's owner greeted him. "I've been so worried about you. Where have you been?" Then she noticed he was all marsh mucky and saltwater sticky. "Oh Skipper, you need a bath!"

While sitting in the tub he thought about his adventure. It was fun, but he was tired. All he wanted to do now was to take a nap and dream about all his new friends.

Did you know...

Osprey migrate to Cape Cod in March to raise a family. In September they all fly south. The family doesn't stay together over the winter. The parents come back individually to the same nest. The younger birds stay down south for an extra year before they return.

Bogs are marshy areas that are made up of peat and sand. This is perfect for growing cranberries.

Tidal marshes are wetlands found along the coast. The amount of salt water in the marsh changes with each tide.

Male fiddler crabs have one big claw to protect themselves and their territory. The female crabs have two small claws.

Heron stand still when they hunt. It makes fish think they are in a safe shady hiding spot.The fish hide around the bird's feet, which then makes them easier to catch.

Horseshoe crabs are closely related to spiders. They were on our planet before the dinosaurs. Their blood is very special and is used in some medicines.

Periwinkles are tiny snails you can find among rocks between high and low tides. They can seal their shells and survive out of water for a long time.

Seagulls aren't picky eaters. They eat fish, crabs, clams . . . insects, spiders, berries . . Burger King, McDonalds, Wendy's and anything else they find.

Sandbars (also known as tidal flats) can be found close to salt marshes. Every day the tide rises and falls, filling in or draining out water. This creates the flat.

Clams survive by burying themselves in the sand. At low tide you can see their small holes. Occasionally they squirt out water which contains waste and sand. They come in hard and soft shells.

Piping plovers are endangered, which means there aren't many left and we need to help keep them safe. Every summer they close off beaches to protect the plover chicks until they can fly off on their own.

The wrack line is made up of shells, seaweed and items caught in the waves. When the tide changes over, the highest waves leave behind a line of everything the wave picked up in its path.

Seaweed is algae. It comes in reds, browns and greens. It also has many shapes and sizes.

Moon snails like to eat clams and other mollusks. If you find a shell with a perfect hole drilled in it, you've found something that was eaten by a moon snail for dinner.

Minnows are small silvery fish that swim in groups. Sometimes there are so many in a group that it looks like a big ball of fish, this is called a "bait ball".

About the Author and Illustrator

Kate Walls is a Cape Cod native who resides in South Yarmouth with her husband and children. Most of her paintings reflect the beauty of the Cape. She creates works in canvas, wood, glass, and paper. Over the past few years she has written and illustrated several children's books. For more information and to view some of her other works, go to www.katewalls.com

Other books:
"Cape Cod Bog Dog", written/illustrated by Kate Walls
"Cape Cod ABCs", written by Leslie Hatton and illustrated by Kate Walls

Go to: www.CapeCodBogDog.com
There you will find coloring sheets, word games, recipes, videos and much more!

Acknowledgements

Thank you to Troy and Macklin for your encouragement while I was creating this book. Thank you to Lyndsay for editing and sharing your expertise in Biology and to Melanie for meticulously pulling everything together. I love you with all of my heart and soul.